Here is Arty – busy painting another masterpiece.

He's the Greatest Artist in the World!

But how did Arty become the Greatest Artist in the World?

LEFT

RIGHT

BUY ONE GET ONE FREE!

The first thing Arty had to do, to become the Greatest Artist in the World, was to order a pair of snowshoes, a nice warm winter coat, and a very tall step ladder.

XS S M L XL

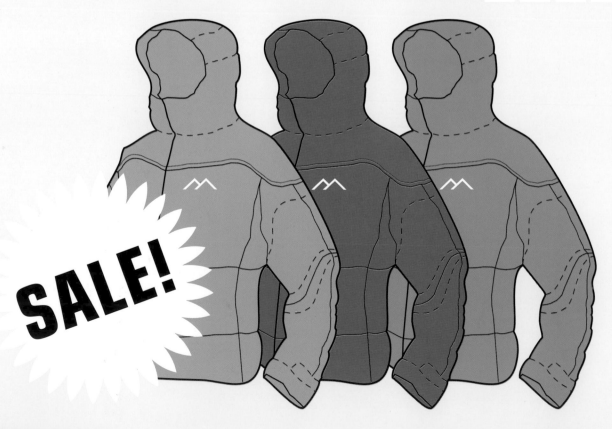

SALE!

Balmoral
H: 2.5 metres

Windsor ▶
H: 0.80 metres

Sandringham ◀
H: 2.0 metres

Kensington ▶
H: 1.25 metres

Highgrove ▶
H: 2.25 metres

EXCLUSIVE STEP LADDER COLLECTION!

The next thing Arty had to do,
to become the Greatest Artist in the World,
was to climb to the top
of the highest mountain in the world –
Mount Everest.

And then,
just to make sure,
Arty climbed to the top
of his step ladder.

And
then
what
did
Arty
do?

He
painted
the
highest
painting
in
the
world!

"And
the
coldest,"
said
Arty.

'After that, I need a couple of weeks lying in bed,' thought Arty.

No such luck!
The next thing Arty had to do,
	to become the Greatest Artist in the World,
	was to climb on to the wing
		of a supersonic jet.

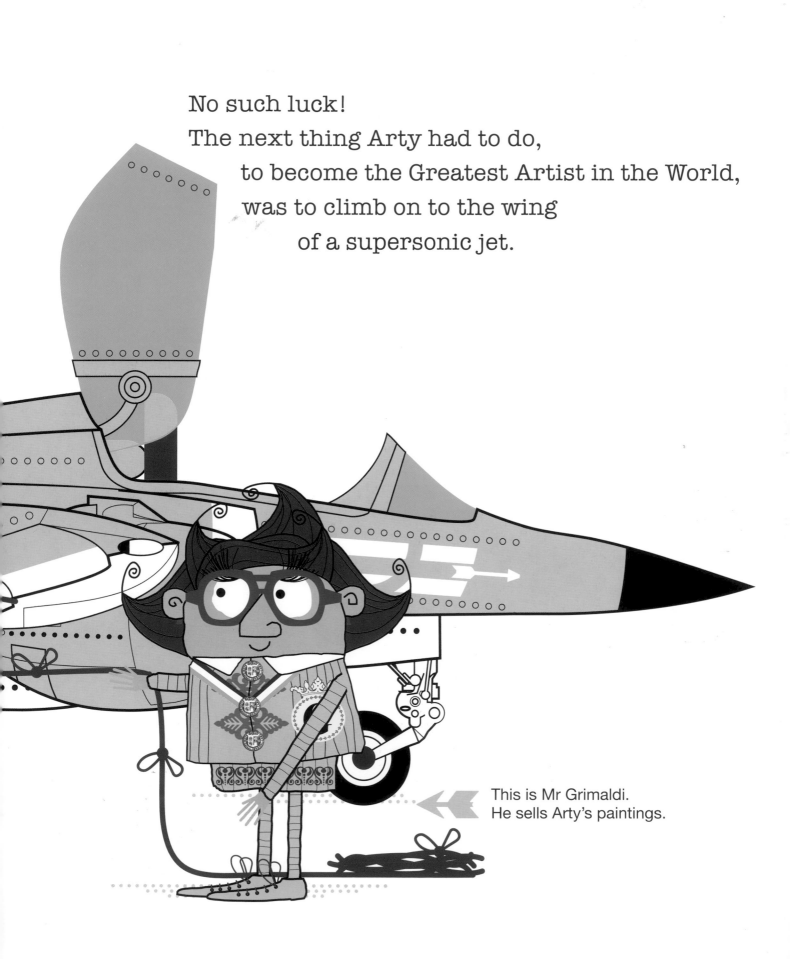

This is Mr Grimaldi.
He sells Arty's paintings.

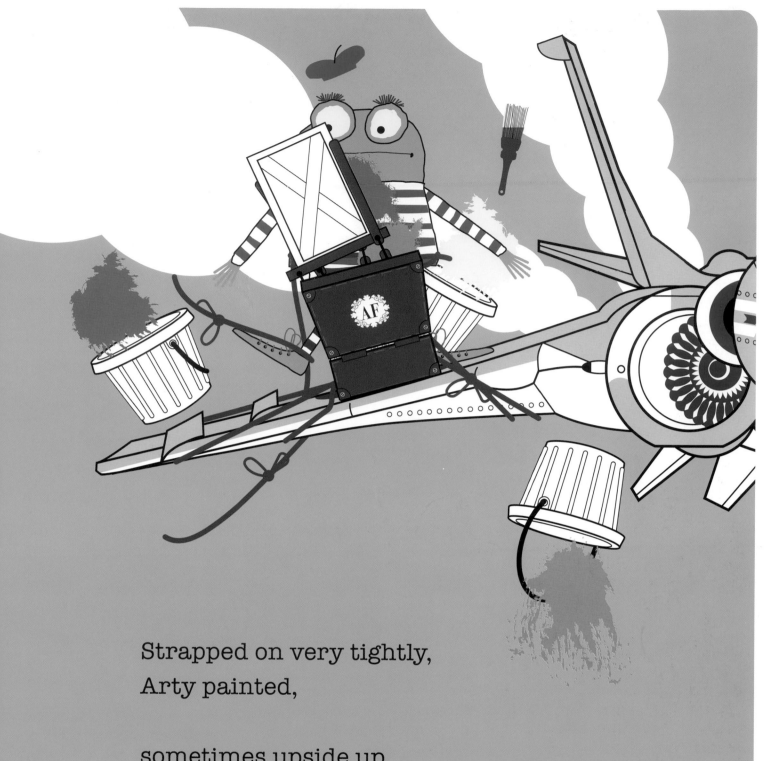

Strapped on very tightly,
Arty painted,

sometimes upside up,
sometimes upside down,
sometimes looping the loop.

It's the *fastest* painting in the world!

After Arty got back down on the ground
he finally spent a couple of weeks lying in bed.

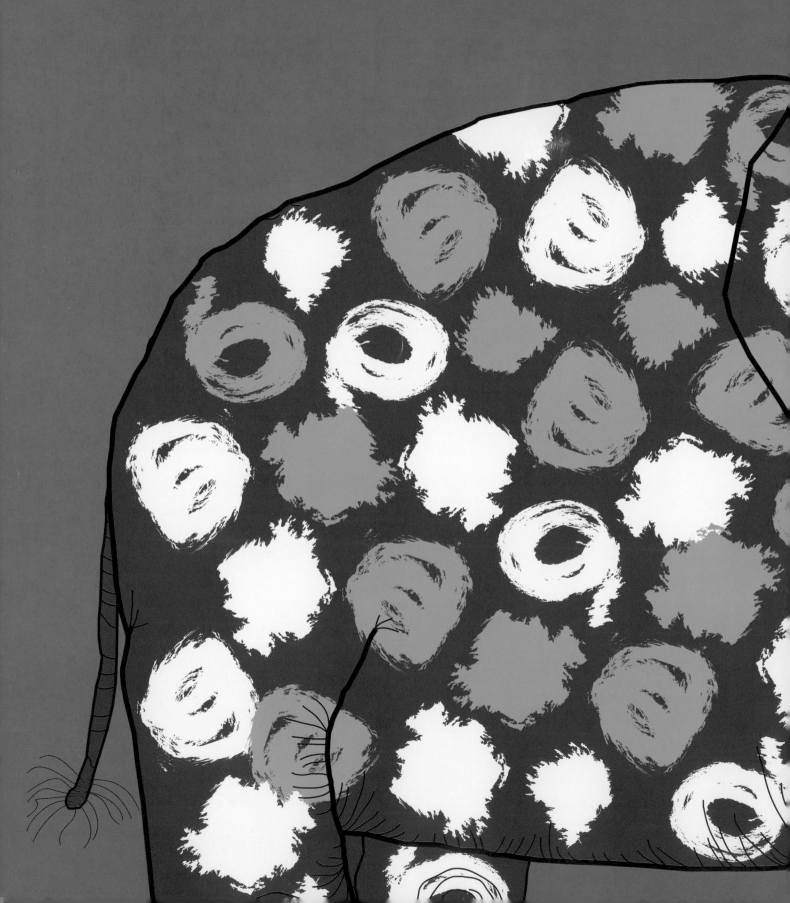

Then he caught up with his friend Tallulah,
and painted the *spottiest* painting in the world!

Next!
Arty painted the *lightest*
painting in the world,

which floated away...

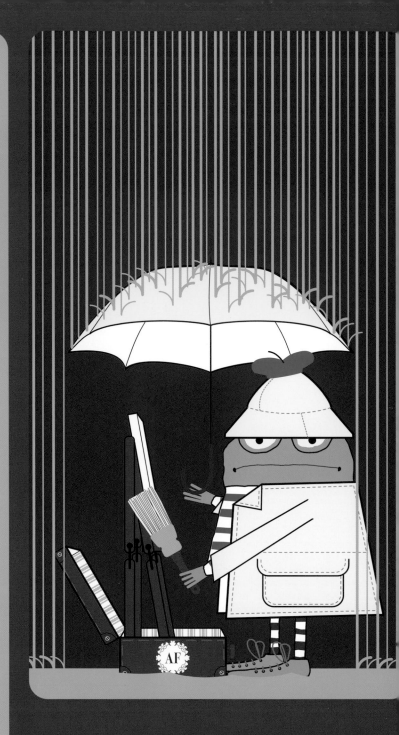

the *wettest* painting
in the world,

and high up
on the highest...

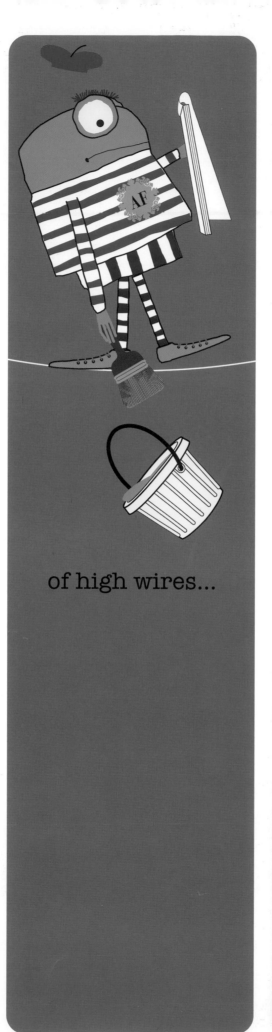

of high wires...

the *wobbliest!*

Then Arty did the next thing he needed to do
to become the Greatest Artist in the World.

He painted as many pictures as he could – all at the same time.

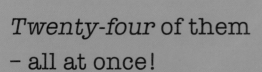

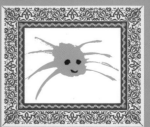

*In fact, it would take THREE artistic octopuses to paint twenty-four pictures – all at once.

Twenty-four of them
– all at once!

"I am like an artistic
octopus!*" said Arty.

Arty loves to play his great big drum.

"This is definitely the *loudest* painting in the world!"
shouted Arty.

And what is this?

"The prettiest painting in the world" said Arty.

The *hairiest* painting in the
world also turned out to be...

"...the *scariest!*" said Arty.

Now if all that doesn't deserve
a couple of weeks lying in bed,
thought Arty, what does?

"YOU CAN LIE IN BED WHEN
YOU ARE THE GREATEST
ARTIST IN THE WORLD!"
shouted Mr Grimaldi

Arty
reluctantly
got out of bed
and climbed
onto a giant
trampoline.

So did
Mr Grimaldi.

Up they both go,
and down they
both go, and up
they both go,
and down they
both go,

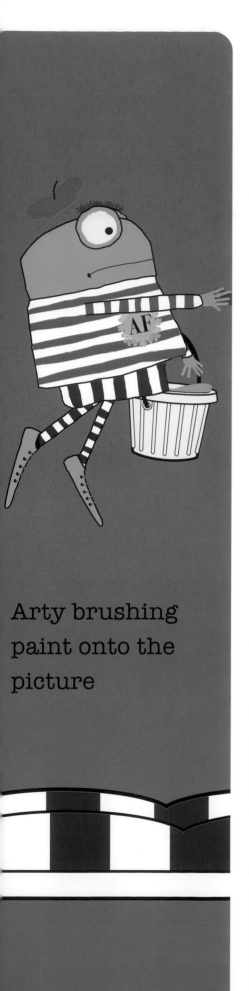

Arty brushing paint onto the picture

whenever he gets anywhere near it.

"This is worse than being strapped to that supersonic jet!" said Arty.

But it's worth it! For the *bounciest* (and *messiest*) painting in the world.

Arty really does need a lie-down now, and so does Mr Grimaldi.

And *that* is how Arty became...

...the GREATEST Artist in the World!

The Greatest Artist in the World

williambee

PAVILION

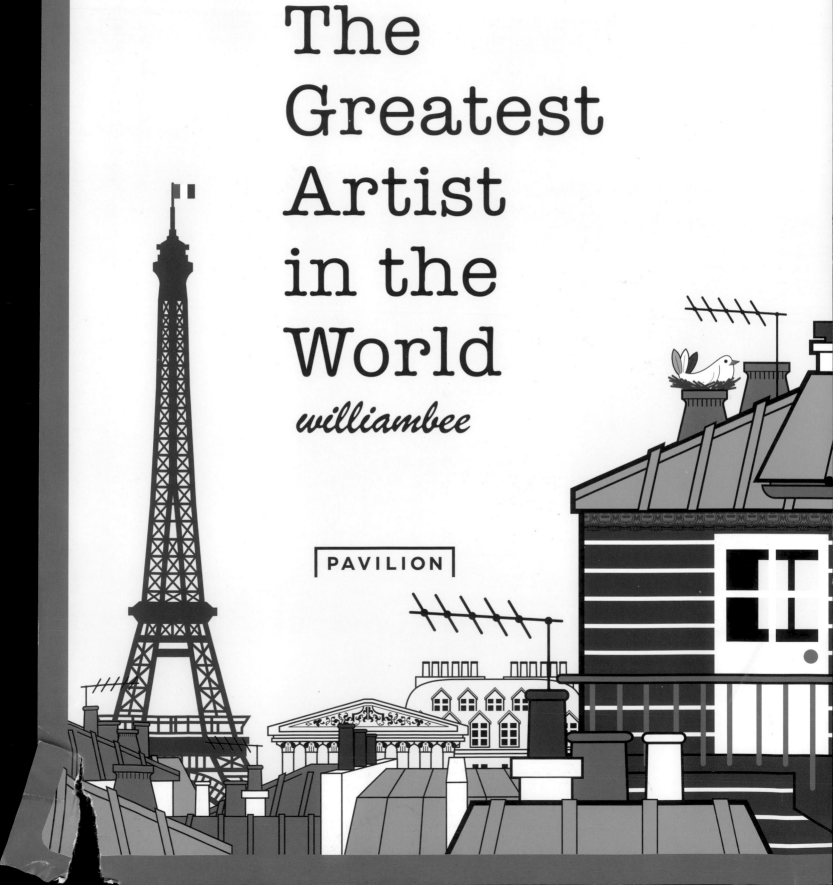

Arty!